D1440416

DARK HUNTER

THE RED THIRST

D1364400

First published 2013 by
A & C Black, an imprint of Bloomsbury Publishing Plc
50 Bedford Square, London, WC1B 3DP

www.bloomsbury.com

Copyright © 2013 A & C Black
Text copyright © 2013 Benjamin Hulme-Cross
Illustrations copyright © 2013 Nelson Evergreen

The right of Benjamin Hulme-Cross and Nelson Evergreen
to be identified as the author and illustrator of this work
has been asserted by them in accordance with
the Copyrights, Designs and Patents Act 1988.

ISBN 978-1-4081-8092-1

A CIP catalogue for this book is available from the British Library.

All rights reserved. No part of this publication may be
reproduced in any form or by any means – graphic, electronic or
mechanical, including photocopying, recording, taping or
information storage and retrieval systems – without the prior per-
mission in writing of the publishers.

Printed and bound by CPI Group (UK) Ltd, Croydon CR0 4YY

1 3 5 7 9 10 8 6 4 2

recommended by

www.catchup.org

Catch Up is a not-for-profit charity
which aims to address the problem of
underachievement that has its roots in
literacy and numeracy difficulties.

DARK HUNTER
THE RED THIRST

BENJAMIN HULME-CROSS
ILLUSTRATED BY NELSON EVERGREEN

A & C BLACK
AN IMPRINT OF BLOOMSBURY
LONDON NEW DELHI NEW YORK SYDNEY

The Dark Hunter

Mr Daniel Blood is the Dark Hunter.
People call him to fight evil demons,
vampires and ghosts.

Edgar and Mary help Mr Blood
with his work.

The three hunters need to be strong and
clever to survive...

ERHAM LIBRARY SERVICE	
B53051359	
Bertrams	09/05/2013
JF	£5.99
AST	

Contents

Contents

Chapter 1

The Coffin

Mr Blood, Mary and Edgar stood in a chapel.

There was a coffin behind them. A dead body lay in the coffin. The dead woman was called Ana.

The villagers had brought Ana's coffin to the chapel and then run away. Only the priest was still there with them.

Mr Blood turned to the priest.

"So, you think there is a vampire in the village. And it feeds on the blood of the dead. Are you quite sure of this?" Mr Blood asked the priest.

"I saw it with my own eyes, sir," said the priest.

The priest was looking at the floor, not at Mr Blood. He said, "I saw it drag a dead body out of the ground last week! That is why we sent for you."

"Very well," said Mr Blood. "Is there a key to the chapel door?"

"No, the key was lost. But there are bolts on the inside. They are very strong," said the priest. "Your helpers must lock themselves inside the chapel. Then they will be safe."

"They will do that," said Mr Blood. "Now you must go, before it gets dark."

The priest turned to leave. "Oh! There is one other thing," he said.

"What is it?" asked Mr Blood.

"I have some food here for you."

The priest handed a sack to Edgar, without looking at him. Then he limped away.

Chapter 2

Stakes

Mary turned to Mr Blood. "Are you going to wait outside to catch the vampire?"

"Yes," said Mr Blood.

"And we will wait in here on our own, with Ana's body?" said Edgar.

"Yes, that is my plan," said Mr Blood.

"But, if this vampire feeds on the blood of the dead…" said Mary.

"And there is a dead body here with us in the chapel…" said Edgar.

"Yes?" Mr Blood snapped.

"Well, the vampire might come for Ana," said Mary.

"Maybe it will," Mr Blood said. "That is why I need you to wait here with the body. But you will be quite safe."

"I hope you are right!" said Edgar.

"Of course you will be safe. That door is the only way into this chapel." Mr Blood pointed at the huge oak door. "And you can bolt the door from inside."

"But we can't lock the door with a key," Edgar said.

Mr Blood ignored him. "You must not let anybody in, apart from me," he said.

"Shouldn't we wait outside with you?" said Mary.

"No," said Mr Blood. "You are safer in here."

"But we want to help you hunt the vampire!" said Mary.

"No, we don't. *I* don't want to sit in a graveyard waiting for a vampire," said Edgar.

"I want you to stay in here. But thank you for the offer, Mary," said Mr Blood.

He gave each of them a large wooden stake. "Take these. Remember, don't let anyone in."

"Yes, we know," said Mary.

"Good," said Mr Blood. "I will watch the graveyard. I will wait for this vampire to come for Ana. When it arrives, I will destroy it."

"So why do we need these stakes?" asked Edgar.

"Just in case something goes wrong. I am being careful, that is all," said Mr Blood.

He went out into the graveyard.

"Make sure you bolt this door behind me," he said.

Edgar and Mary stood in the doorway with Ana's open coffin behind them.

Mr Blood looked among the gravestones for a place to hide.

Chapter 3

Waiting

"I wonder what Ana was like," said Mary.

She took some bread and cheese out of the bag the priest had left. Edgar bolted the door.

"Do you want something to eat?" said Mary, with her mouth full.

Edgar slid the last bolt into place. He turned around. "Are you *eating*?"

"Mmm," mumbled Mary. "Do you want some?"

"No, I do not!" said Edgar. He lit a candle. "How can you stand there, next to a dead body, and stuff your face?"

Mary didn't care. "I wonder if Ana knew her body was going to be used as bait," she said.

"Never mind her, she's dead!" said Edgar. "What about us?"

He went around the chapel, and lit all the candles he could find.

"Us?" Mary snorted. "We're not bait! The priest said this vampire only feeds on the dead."

"How does he know?" said Edgar. "Maybe the vampire feeds on the dead because they don't fight back. Maybe it really prefers hot blood from living people."

"Yes, who ever heard of a vampire that prefers dead blood?" said Mary. "Maybe it will come for us after all!"

She smiled and popped a piece of cheese in her mouth.

"I have a bad feeling about this," said Edgar. "Why do Mr Blood's plans always put us in danger?"

He walked up and down. "This vampire is going to come looking for a dead body. And it's going to find us. And when that happens, it's going to think that it has been missing out on nice warm blood."

"Yes, and it will attack us! Fun, isn't it?" said Mary.

Edgar shook his head. "It's dark outside. I bet the vampire is on its way here now."

"I wish I was out there with Mr Blood," said Mary.

"I don't know why you say these things," said Edgar. "You know we're safer in here."

"But I want to go out there and catch vampires!" said Mary. "I want to see what happens. I want to know how to do it."

"Why?" asked Edgar. "It's so scary!"

"Mr Blood is never scared," said Mary. "And he always wins, no matter what the danger is."

She waved her dagger. "Don't you see? That's what I want to be like. I want to be fearless and get rid of vampires and monsters and anything else that is evil."

"I just want us to live," said Edgar. "Every time we do one of these jobs, I get to the end of it and wonder how I'm still alive."

"Well, we are in no more danger than anyone in the village." Mary gave a big yawn.

"We are guarding a dead body so she can be buried," she went on. "If we don't do it, who will? The people here won't do it. They would not look any of us in the eye. Even the priest couldn't look at us."

"They were weird," said Edgar.

"They were scared," said Mary. She yawned again and then bit into an apple.

Edgar walked over to one of the
windows and looked out.

Any of the shadows could have hidden
a vampire. There was no sign of
Mr Blood. The wind rattled the windows.

Chapter 4

Sleepy

Mary lay down on the stone floor.

"Edgar, do you mind if I rest for a few minutes?" she asked.

"*What?*" Edgar shouted. "You want to sleep? A minute ago you wanted to go out and fight vampires! What is wrong with you?"

But Mary was already asleep. Edgar shook her and shouted at her but he could not wake her.

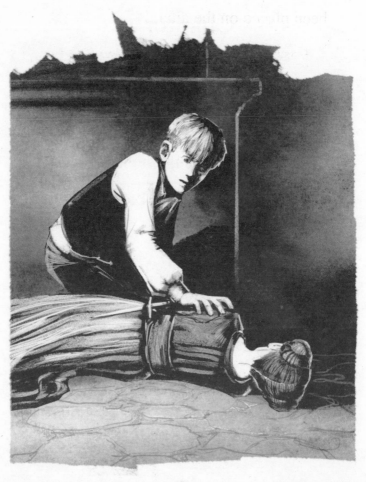

"This is just like her," Edgar said to himself. "Now what?"

He went over to the open coffin. It had been placed on the altar.

For the first time he saw how lovely Ana was. She had jet black hair, very pale skin and dark red lips. Shadows danced across her face as the candle flames flickered.

It almost looked as if Ana was moving, Edgar thought.

A sudden shout outside made Edgar jump. He rushed to the window and looked out. He saw a dark figure racing away from the chapel. Mr Blood was chasing it.

Edgar went over to the door to check the bolts.

He heard the sound of a key turning in the lock.

Somebody had just locked the door, from the outside.

Now Edgar and Mary were trapped in the chapel with Ana's body. And Mr Blood was locked out.

Edgar put his ear to the door. He heard whispers.

"They should both be asleep. Did you make them eat the drugged food?" said a voice.

"I couldn't force it down their throats. I gave them a bag with it in," came a second whisper. It was the priest.

So that was why Mary fell asleep, thought Edgar. *The food was drugged! But why? And where is Mr Blood now?*

Chapter 5

Awake

Edgar ran over to Mary and shook her.
"Wake up! Please wake up!" he hissed.
But still she slept.

Edgar looked up at the window and saw
a small flash of light.

He stood up. There was the flash again. But it was too quick for Edgar to see anything.

He put his nose against the glass.

A torch flared into light outside. On the other side of the window was the face of the priest. He was looking right at Edgar.

Edgar jumped back, and crashed into a jug of water. It smashed. Water poured out all over the floor, and all over Mary's face.

A piece of the broken jug fell onto Mary's arm. The sharp edge cut her skin. Blood ran down her arm.

She moved a little in her sleep.

Outside the window, Edgar could see a crowd of villagers. They began to chant. The crowd were looking at something behind Edgar.

Edgar felt shivers run down his back .

He turned around and screamed.

Ana was standing next to the altar. She smiled at Edgar. Her teeth were long, slim fangs. Slowly, she began to walk towards him.

Where is Mr Blood? thought Edgar. *He must know by now that we have been fooled. The villagers do not want to be rid of a vampire. They are helping a vampire!*

Chapter 6

Hunting

Edgar picked up his wooden stake and tried to hit Ana.

She brushed him off with one arm. She was very strong.

The blow sent Edgar flying across the chapel. He crashed into the window. It broke.

He got up and began to move around the floor, holding the wooden stake in front of him.

Ana came closer and closer. Then she stopped right by Mary's body.

Ana's face changed. She took a deep breath and her eyes became slits.

She looked down and saw the trickle of blood that was coming from Mary's arm.

Ana knelt down and put her mouth to the blood. She began to lick. It was as if she could not think about anything else.

Edgar heard a shout from outside. "Now, Edgar! Now! This is your only chance!" It was Mr Blood.

Ana was still licking up Mary's blood. Edgar crept across the floor. Ana had her back to him.

Edgar raised the wooden stake over Ana
and brought it down hard.

The wood went through Ana's back, and into her heart.

She gave a moan of agony and struggled to her feet.

She staggered backwards, falling among the candles.

Her dress brushed across one of the candle flames and caught fire.

Ana fell into her coffin face down and lay still. Soon the whole coffin was in flames.

Edgar stood by the window, shaking.

He looked out. There was no more chanting.

The villagers looked worn out and confused. It was as if they had just woken up from a bad dream.

The vampire's spell was broken!

One by one they turned and began to walk slowly away until only Mr Blood was left.

"Well done, my boy! Very, very well done!" Mr Blood said, clapping his hands.

Edgar could not speak. Mary sat up slowly and rubbed her eyes. "Did I miss anything?" she said.

Edgar glared at her. "Did you miss anything?" he croaked. "Did you *miss* anything? That is just like you!"